The Show-Off

Story by Carmel Reilly
Illustrations by Pat Reynolds

Contents

Chapter 1	At the Gym	2
Chapter 2	Choosing the Team	6
Chapter 3	The Game	14
Chapter 4	Team Players	20

HOUGHTON MIFFLIN HARCOURT
Supplemental Publishers

www.Rigby.com
800-531-5015

Chapter 1
At the Gym

"Wow," said Eddie as he arrived for his first training session with the Junior Superstars. "This place is enormous!"

Brad Hill, Eddie's new coach, grinned. "We have five courts here at the gym," he said, "so there's a lot of room for all our teams to practice."

Eddie stood with his dad and his friend, Nina, and waited for the other players to arrive.

Nina nudged Eddie. "Look," she said. "There's that boy, Dylan, we met at the park a while ago. He must be on the team, too."

At the Gym

3

The Show-Off

Eddie turned around and watched Dylan and his dad as they went to talk to Brad Hill. Eddie remembered that Dylan's dad used to play for the City Superstars when he was younger.

"It's not going to be much fun playing with Dylan," Eddie said, groaning. "He's an amazing player, but he is such a show-off."

"Brad wouldn't have chosen him if he didn't think he could work with the team," Eddie's dad reassured him.

"I hope so," said Nina.

At the Gym

Chapter 2
Choosing the Team

Brad Hill called the players over.

"Welcome to the Junior Superstars, everyone," he said. "Today I need to choose the main players for the team this Saturday. We'll have a practice game now so I can see how you all work together."

Brad put the children onto two teams. "You five are on one side," he said, "and you five are on the other side."

Eddie's heart sank when he saw that he was going to be on the same side as Dylan.

Choosing the Team

The Show-Off

The game started, and one of the girls threw the ball to Eddie. But Dylan swooped between them and grabbed it.

He ran quickly, dribbled the ball to the other end, and scored. He yelled loudly and punched the air.

A little later, Eddie had the ball and was dribbling it to the end of the court. But before he could aim at the basket, Dylan snatched the ball from him and took a shot. He whooped and yelled as the ball flew through the hoop.

Choosing the Team

The Show-Off

Choosing the Team

After a few minutes, Brad blew his whistle. "Let's take a break," he said.

Nina ran over to talk to Eddie. "I can't believe what Dylan is doing. He grabs the ball all the time, even when he doesn't need to," she said.

"I know," said Eddie. "It's really annoying. And Brad will probably think Dylan is better than everyone else because he's always in the middle of the play."

The Show-Off

At the end of practice, Brad called everyone over. He was about to tell them who would be the main players on Saturday, when Dylan called out.

"Brad! What position will I have?" he asked.

Brad frowned. "You're a good player, Dylan," he said. "But you need to work more with the others before you are ready to play on the main team. This Saturday, I want you to be a substitute."

Dylan looked shocked.

"Now for this week, I would like to see these people on the court," said Brad, calling out five names. Eddie leapt up when he heard he was one of them.

Chapter 3
The Game

Eddie arrived at the gym early on Saturday morning. He was surprised to see Dylan already waiting there. Eddie walked over to him.

"Are you all right?" he asked.

"I wish I was playing today," Dylan said sadly. "At practice, I was trying so hard to impress everyone that I forgot about teamwork."

"Your dad was a great team player," said Eddie.

"I know," said Dylan. "I wish I could show him today that I really can play well on a team."

The Game

The Show-Off

A few minutes into the game, Bella, who was playing center, tripped and fell. The players gathered around as Brad helped her back to the bench.

"We need someone to take Bella's place," said Brad. He looked at the players on the bench. For a moment, he looked straight at Dylan, but then he moved on.

"Harry, can you go in now?" Brad asked.

The Game

17

The Show-Off

At halftime, the team was down by eight points and some of the children were starting to look tired.

Dylan put his hand up. "Please, can I go in for a while?" he asked. "I could give someone a rest."

"I know he'll play well," said Eddie.

Brad looked hard at Dylan. "All right, Dylan, you can give Mara a break," he said finally.

Dylan took a deep breath and ran onto the court.

The Game

19

Chapter 4

Team Players

Eddie chased the other team's center player as he dribbled the ball down the court. The center passed the ball to another player, but Eddie zipped across in front of him and snatched it.

To his left, Eddie could see Dylan waving his arms. Eddie quickly flipped the ball up and over the heads of the other team. Dylan jumped up, grabbed the ball, and ran.

Moments later, he had scored.

Team Players

The Show-Off

Eddie raced back to defend at the other end. As the ball rebounded off the backboard, he leapt high to catch it.

Soon the ball was back down to Dylan. He aimed at the basket.

But as Eddie appeared, Dylan quickly passed the ball to him. Eddie scored!

Dylan gave Eddie a high five. "That was great!" he said.

"I couldn't have done it without you," Eddie replied.

Team Players

The Show-Off

At the end of the game, Brad spoke to the team.

"I was very happy with the way you all played today, especially Eddie and Dylan," he said.

Dylan and Eddie grinned at each other.

"I think you both got to show off your talents in the best possible way," Brad added, "as team players."